Yikes-Lice!

Donna Caffey

illustrations by **Patrick Girouard**

www.av2books.com

Your AV² Media Enhanced book gives you a fiction readalong online. Log on to www.av2books.com and enter the unique book code from this page to use your readalong.

AV² Readalong Navigation

HIGHLIGHTED TEXT

HOME

CLOSE

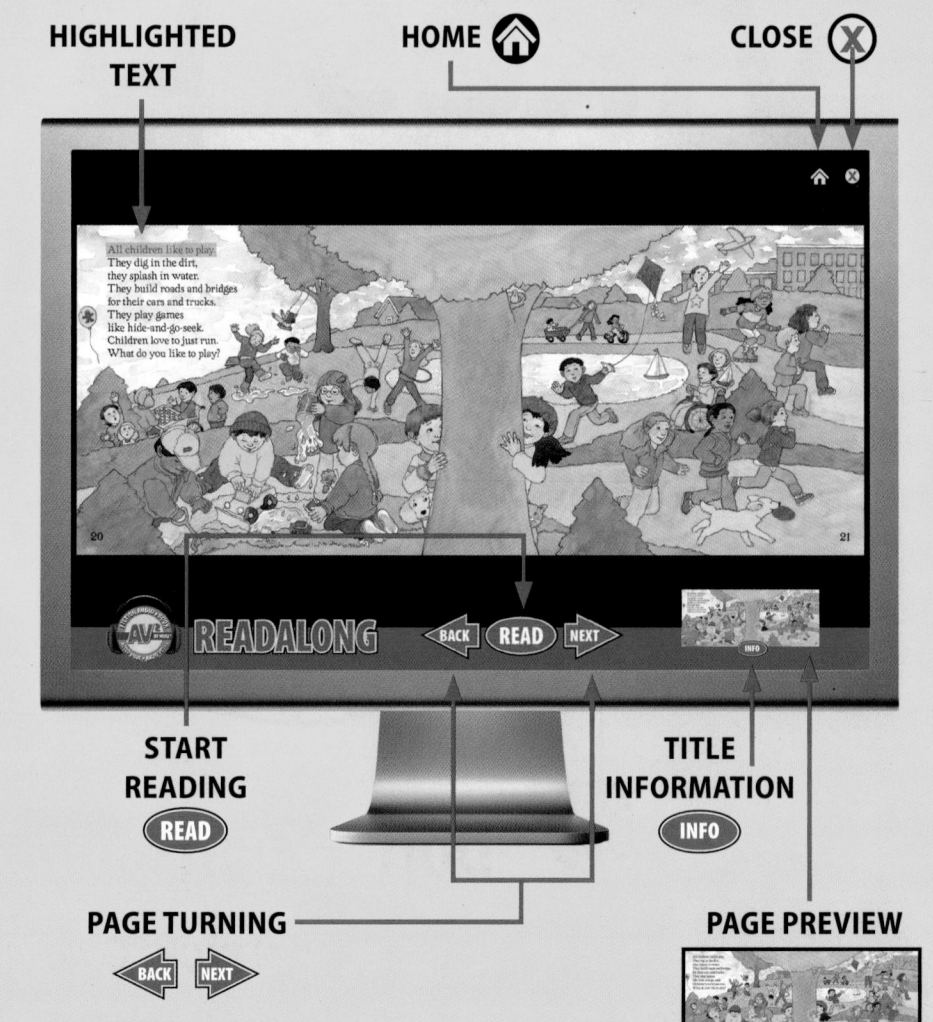

START READING READ

PAGE TURNING BACK NEXT

TITLE INFORMATION INFO

PAGE PREVIEW

Go to **www.av2books.com**, and enter this book's unique code.

BOOK CODE

S504267

AV² by Weigl brings you media enhanced books that support active learning.

First Published by

ALBERT WHITMAN & COMPANY
Publishing children's books since 1919

Published by AV² by Weigl
350 5ᵗʰ Avenue, 59ᵗʰ Floor New York, NY 10118
Website: www.av2books.com   www.weigl.com

Library of Congress Control Number: 2013940836

ISBN 978-1-62127-912-9 (hardcover)
ISBN 978-1-48961-503-9 (single-user eBook)
ISBN 978-1-48961-504-6 (multi-user eBook)

Printed in the United States of America in North Mankato, Minnesota
1 2 3 4 5 6 7 8 9 0 17 16 15 14 13

Text copyright ©1998 by Donna Jaye Caffey.
Illustrations copyright ©1998 by Patrick Girouard.
Published in 1998 by Albert Whitman & Company.

052013
WEP250413

A note to Concerned Grownups

People sometimes think that head lice are a sign of uncleanliness, but in fact anyone, no matter how clean, can get them. They are easily passed by being in close contact with someone or by sharing combs, brushes, or hats. It can be irritating and disturbing to feel head lice on your scalp, but they are not known to carry any human disease.

Young children have higher rates of head lice infestation than older children and adults. Children between the ages of three and ten are the most likely to get them. In this age group, boys and girls tend to be at equal risk. Among teenagers, girls are more often affected than boys. White children are more likely to get head lice than are African-American children.

Desperate parents have tried many household remedies, some of them dangerous and all of them unproven. Children have occasionally been seriously harmed from these home remedies, which have included commercial pesticides, kerosene, and gasoline.

Several treatments are available in pharmacies, over-the-counter, or by prescription. Some studies have suggested that lice may be gaining resistance to some of these treatments. I have been participating in a current study to determine whether available treatments are still as effective as they once were in the United States. Until research gives us new answers, the best way to deal with lice is to carefully follow the instructions given in the lice treatment packages, taking care to thoroughly remove all the lice and nits.

And remember, although head lice are a nuisance, they are not something to be feared.

Christine G. Hahn, M.D.

A cootie with an attitude
crept forth one day in search of food.
I'm starvin'!

The head louse, sometimes called a cootie, lives on the human head. It is a wingless insect 1/16 to 1/8 inch long, about the size of a pinhead. Head lice (the plural of louse) range in color from light brown to dark brown or black. They do not live on animals. A head louse crawls, but it does not hop, jump, or fly.

She hitched a ride on someone's comb
and went to find a great new home.
Thanks for the lift!

Tired and hungry, she saw some food;
a yummy meal soon changed her mood.
Mmmm!

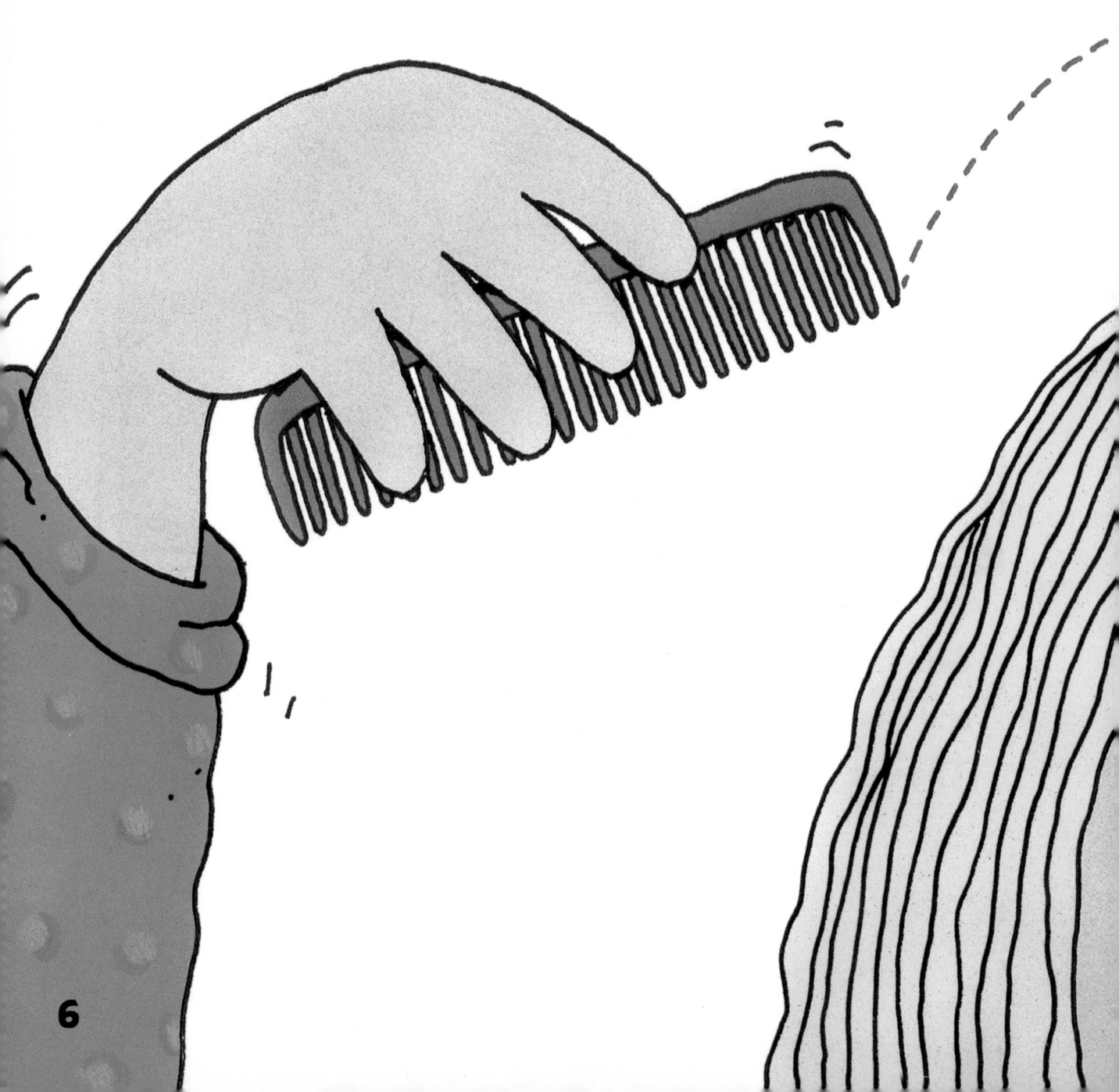

Lice are usually found nestled in the hair close to the scalp at the top of the head, behind the ears, or at the back of the neck. They have six legs, with claws used for holding onto hair.

Lice require blood from the "host," or human being they are living on, in order to survive. They use their sucking mouth parts to pierce the skin and feed. If left alone, lice will feed quickly and frequently. Without a meal, they cannot live more than one or two days.

She raised a family right away.
Those kids played hide and seek all day.
Ready or not, here I come!

The female louse can lay 3 to 6 eggs per day—about 5o to 150 in her lifetime. The eggs, called nits, are very small (about 1/32 of an inch in length), oval-shaped, and grayish-white. The female attaches the nits to hair with a gummy substance.

Her little ones grew up quite quick,
had tykes themselves, and stayed real thick.
A family reunion!

It takes seven to ten days for a nit to hatch and the young louse, or nymph, to emerge. Soon the nymphs mature into adults. Then the female can lay eggs of her own. Most lice live about a month, long enough to have many children and grandchildren.

Meanwhile—

my head began to creep and crawl

with these intruders weird and small.

What was up?

If your head itches a lot, you should be checked for lice! The itching is caused by the feeding louse who punctures the skin, injects saliva, and then sucks blood. However, you can have lice and not itch.

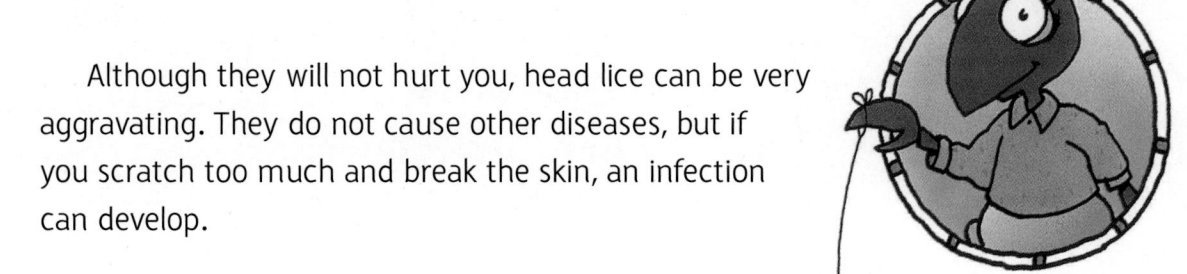

**I scratched my head from neck to top.
It itched so much I couldn't stop!
Ugh!**

Although they will not hurt you, head lice can be very aggravating. They do not cause other diseases, but if you scratch too much and break the skin, an infection can develop.

I yelled at Mom to come and look.
She grabbed a light. She glared, then shook!
Yikes!

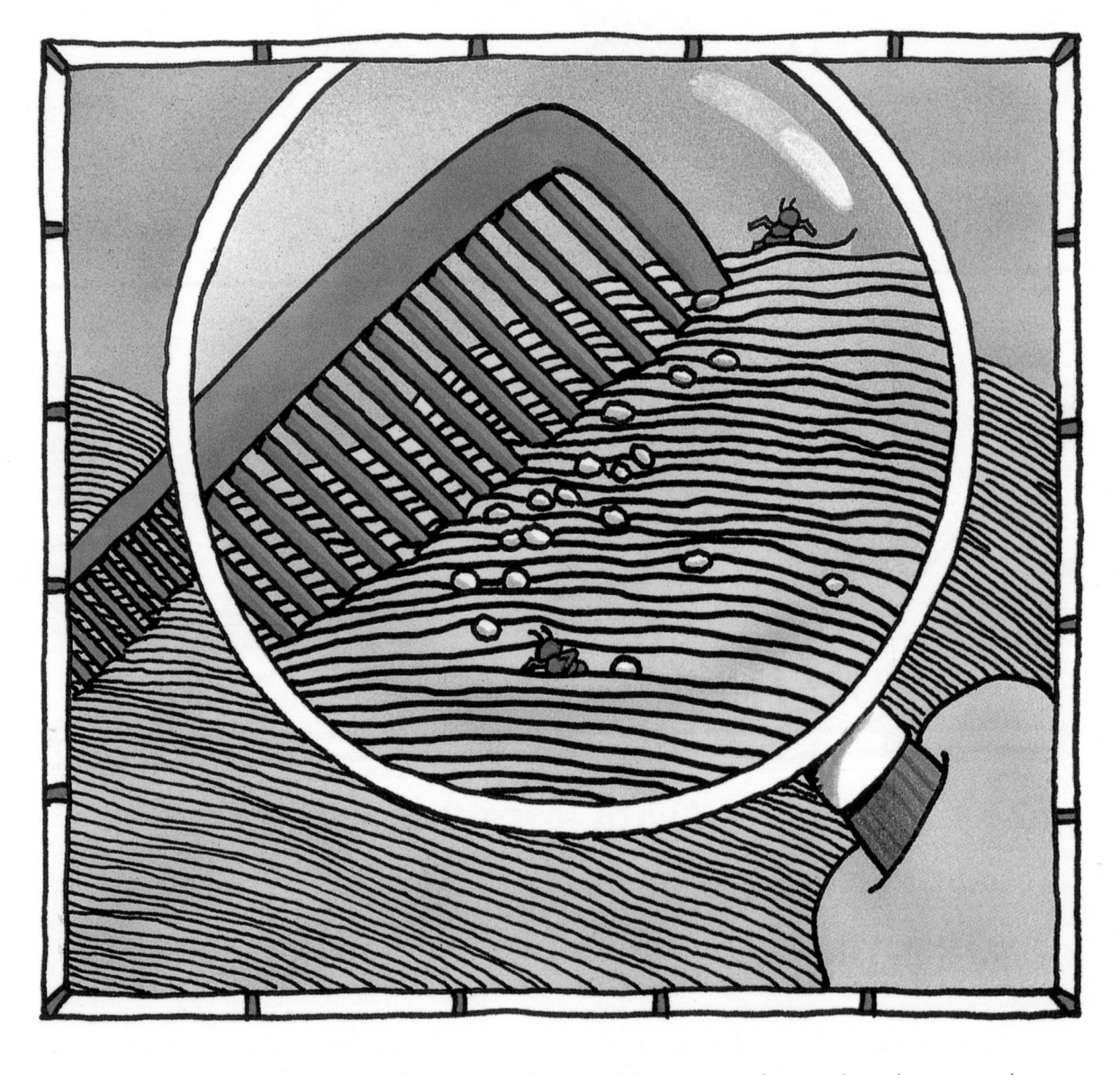

You will need help to check yourself for head lice. Lean forward under a good light. The "checker" can use a comb with a tail to part and lift the hair. He or she should begin at the back of the neck and proceed to each side, lifting the hair in small sections all over the head. Most lice and nits can be seen with the naked eye, but a magnifying glass might be helpful. (Be sure everyone's hands and all the equipment are washed after the examination.)

She soaped my head with louse shampoo.

It zapped those pests. I yelled, "Yahoo!"

You're outta here!

If you have lice, your hair can be washed with a louse-killing shampoo or rinse. There are several kinds you can buy. The instructions on the package should be carefully followed. If you have questions, ask your doctor. Anyone who has been in close contact with a person with lice should also be checked for lice.

She combed my hair out over a towel;
the snarls and tangles made me growl.
OUCH!

All the nits must be removed from your hair. Otherwise, they'll hatch and you'll have more lice. You'll need someone to help you get the nits out. The helper should use a nit-removal comb (these combs are often sold with lice shampoo) and work one section of hair at a time. It may be easier for someone to use his or her fingers to pull out the sticky, seedlike nits.

Combing out nits can take awhile, so be patient! It's very important to get every single one.

**Dad pitched in to start the chore
of cleaning stuff we shouldn't ignore.
Even Ole Blue!**

   To make sure that lice are completely gone, everything that
was exposed must be thoroughly cleaned. Personal items such as combs, brushes,
and hair accessories must be soaked in very hot (but not boiling) water for twenty
minutes. Clothing, linens, and towels should be washed with hot soapy water and
completely dried in a clothes dryer using the hot cycle. Nonwashable items such
as some stuffed animals, pillows, bedspreads, bike helmets, and headsets with
foam earpieces, should be dry-cleaned or placed in an airtight plastic bag
for two weeks.

PLASTIC BAGS

He swept the sofa, chairs, and rugs, to clean our house of all stray bugs. Whew!

Because lice can live from one to two days away from a person, sofas, chairs, mattresses, carpets, and car upholstery should be thoroughly vacuumed. Throw the vacuum bag away.

But you do not need to spray the house with insecticides. Remember that lice don't live long away from people, and you do not want to expose yourself to unnecessary chemicals.

Our work complete, we had a chat.
Dad warned me not to share my hat.
No way!

Often people get lice in schools and camps or anywhere they are in close contact. It helps if you do not share your combs, brushes, hats, helmets, headsets, or clothes. If you do get lice, you should tell your teachers and friends so they can be checked. You should be checked again every day for two weeks and regularly after that.

**Mom said, "You don't deserve the blame.
It's not your fault those cooties came."
That's right!**

It's not your fault if you get head lice—anyone can! According to historians, head lice have been around for nine thousand years. They have been found on people of all races all over the world, no matter where they are living or how clean they are.

We fought and won the war on lice;
without them, life is supernice!
Give me five!